STECK-VAUGHN

PAIR-IT BOOKS™

Bats at Bat

Written by Christine Price
Illustrated by John Gieg

STECK-VAUGHN
®
C O M P A N Y
ELEMENTARY • SECONDARY • ADULT • LIBRARY

What if bats could bat?

2

What if ducks could duck?

3

What if horses could get hoarse?

What if hares could cut hair?

What if slides could slide?

What if flies could fly?

Hey, flies CAN fly!

8